RAT RIDD

Also in the Animal Ark Pets Series

LUCY DANIELS
Rat
Riddle

Illustrated by Paul Howard

Hodder
Children's
Books

a division of Hodder Headline plc

Special thanks to Linda Chapman

Animal Ark is a trademark of Ben M. Baglio
Text copyright © 1999 Ben M. Baglio
Created by Ben M. Baglio, London W12 7QY
Illustrations copyright © 1999 Paul Howard
Cover illustration by Chris Chapman

First published in Great Britain in 1999
by Hodder Children's Books

The right of Lucy Daniels to be identified as the Author of
this Work has been asserted by her in accordance with the
Copyright, Designs and Patents Act 1988.

10 9 8 7 6 5 4 3 2 1

All rights reserved. No part of this publication may be reproduced,
stored in a retrieval system, or transmitted, in any form or by any
means without the prior written permission of the publisher, nor be
otherwise circulated in any form of binding or cover other than that
in which it is published and without a similar condition being
imposed on the subsequent purchaser.

All characters in this publication are fictitious and any resemblance
to real persons, living or dead, is purely coincidental.

A Catalogue record for this book is available from the British Library

ISBN 0 340 73590 2

Typeset by Avon Dataset Ltd, Bidford-on-Avon, Warks

Printed and bound in Great Britain by
The Guernsey Press Co. Ltd, Channel Isles

Hodder Children's Books
a division of Hodder Headline plc
338 Euston Road
London NW1 3BH

Contents

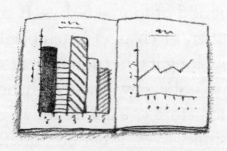

1

The homework project

Mrs Todd clapped her hands for quiet. "Shut your books now, Class Five," she said. "I want to tell you about your next homework project."

Mandy Hope finished the last label on her graph, then shut her maths book and looked up at her teacher.

1

"It's a maths project this time," Mrs Todd told her class. "I want you to find something that you can record on a graph, over a period of fourteen days. It could be the weather, or changes in temperature, or even how long it takes you to get to school each day." She saw Mandy's hand shoot up. "And before you ask, Mandy," she said with a smile, "yes, it *can* be something to do with animals."

Mandy grinned. She loved animals. When she grew up she wanted to be a vet – just like her mum and dad. They had a veterinary practice called Animal Ark.

Jill Redfern, who sat next to Mandy, looked pleased. "That's good. I can record how long it takes Toto to get to his feeding bowl each day." Toto was Jill's tortoise.

"And I can see how long it takes for Sooty, my puppy, to *eat* his food each day," said Sarah Drummond, another of Mandy's friends.

"About two seconds!" joked Jill. "What will you do, Mandy?"

Mandy didn't know. Her mum and dad were too busy looking after other people's animals to let her have a pet of her own. Maybe she could record something that happened at Animal Ark. What about how many patients came in each day, or . . . ?

Mrs Todd's voice interrupted her thoughts. "I want your graphs, along with a written description of what you have been measuring and what you have found, to be handed in three weeks on Monday." The school bell rang. Mrs Todd clapped her hands. "Time for assembly. Line up, please."

Class Five followed Mrs Todd down the corridor. As they went into the hall, Mandy saw her best friend, James Hunter, sitting with his class. James was a year younger than Mandy, and was in Class Four. He waved at her and she hurried to sit just behind him. "We've got a maths project to do for homework," she told him. "And it can be about—"

Just then Mrs Garvie, the Headteacher,

stood up on the platform. "Good morning, everybody," she said.

"Good morning, Mrs Garvie," the whole school chorused, and assembly began.

At the end of every assembly, Mrs Garvie announced any birthdays in the school. Today, her eyes fell on a skinny boy with blond hair who was sitting just along the row from James. "We have a birthday in Class Four today," Mrs Garvie announced. "It is Martin Adams's ninth birthday. Happy birthday, Martin! Would you like to stand up?"

Martin Adams stood up. His cheeks were red and he stared hard at the floor, his fair hair falling down over his face. Mandy looked at him curiously. She didn't know Martin very well. He was quite shy, and now – with everyone's attention on him – he was looking as if he wanted the floor to open up and swallow him.

"Have you had any nice presents for your birthday, Martin?" Mrs Garvie asked, smiling at him.

Martin looked up. For one moment his eyes brightened and his face seemed to shine with excitement. Mandy leaned forward with interest. She wondered what he was going to say.

There was a pause. "Well?" Mrs Garvie asked him again, gently.

Martin looked round at the people sitting near him and the excitement suddenly seemed to vanish from his face. "I got a jumper," he mumbled, looking at the floor again. "And a pair of trainers."

Mandy sat back, disappointed. A jumper and a pair of trainers! That wasn't very interesting. She'd thought he had been going to say something *really* exciting. She looked at Martin as he sat back down. It was almost as though he had been about to say something else and then changed his mind. Mandy felt curious.

"James," she said at break, "what's Martin Adams like?"

James peeled his orange. "He's really quiet. He doesn't sit on my table. I had to do a computer project with him once, but he didn't say much." He pushed back his thick, brown hair. "So, what's this maths project you have to do for homework?"

Mandy pushed Martin to the back of her mind and explained. "I want to think of something to do with Animal Ark," she said after she had filled James in on the details.

"There are loads of things you could record," James said enthusiastically. He liked maths. "How about counting how many cats come in for their vaccinations, or how many different types of animals come in over the fourteen days?"

The bell rang for the end of break. "Will you help me think about it over the weekend?" asked Mandy. "I want it to be really good."

James nodded. "Of course!" He set off for his classroom. "See you later."

When school finished, they met by the bike shed. James was going back with Mandy to Animal Ark for tea. They were just wheeling their bikes down the school path when Martin Adams came hurrying past. "Bye, Martin!" James called. But Martin didn't look round – he just ran down to the school gate, where his mum was waiting for him. James looked at Mandy in surprise. "He's in a hurry," he commented.

"Maybe he's having a birthday party or something," Mandy suggested.

James frowned. "I haven't seen him give out any invitations."

Mandy shrugged, her thoughts turning to the animals that would be waiting for them at Animal Ark. "I wonder how many animals will be in the surgery today," she said. "I can't wait to see!"

They cycled off through the village, finally reaching Animal Ark and swerving up the driveway together. Leaving their bikes outside the old stone cottage where Mandy and her parents lived, they went round to the modern veterinary surgery attached on to the back.

Jean Knox, the receptionist, was tapping away at the computer keyboard and peering through her glasses at the screen. She looked up and smiled at them. "How was school?" she asked.

"Fine," Mandy replied. "I've got to do a maths project. It's going to be about animals. Are Mum and Dad here? I want to tell them about it."

"Your dad's on call, but your mum's in the residential unit," Jean told her. The residential unit was where the animals stayed when they were recovering from operations or were too sick to go home.

Mrs Hope was just closing the door of one of the cat cages when Mandy and James bounced in. "Hello, you two," she said, a warm smile lighting up her green eyes.

"Hi, Mum," said Mandy. She looked closely at the cat in the cage. "Isn't that the cat who lives next door to Gran and Grandad?" she asked.

Mrs Hope nodded. "He's been fighting.

Nothing too serious, but he did need some stitches in his ear. Now he's just waiting to go home."

The cat glared at Mandy and James. It obviously didn't like being in a cage. "You poor thing," Mandy said to him. "Never mind. You'll be home soon."

"Come and see this little fellow," Mrs Hope said, taking them over to a cage where a golden hamster was snuffling through a layer of wood shavings. He was round and fat and his coat was the colour of honey. Mrs Hope took him out. "Would you like to hold him, James?" she asked, with a smile. She knew James liked animals almost as much as Mandy did.

"Yes, please." James eagerly took the hamster and cuddled him close. "He's lovely. What's he called?" he asked.

"Sandy," Mrs Hope replied.

Mandy stroked Sandy's head with the tip of one finger. His fur felt like velvet. "What's the matter with him, Mum?"

"Someone fed him a toffee," said Mrs Hope. "And it got stuck to the inside of his pouches. We had to flush them out, but he's fine now." She smiled and took the little hamster off James. "Although he'll have to do without sticky sweets from now on, won't you, Sandy?"

After she had put the hamster back in his cage, Mrs Hope washed her hands at the sink. "I'm going into Walton to get a few things. Do you two want to come with me?"

Mandy looked at James. He nodded. "Yes, please," Mandy said. "I need to get some more birdseed for the garden."

They piled into the back of Mrs Hope's four-wheel drive. "We can get the birdseed from the hardware shop," Mrs Hope said. "I have to call in there anyway, to get a washer for the kitchen tap."

Mandy remembered that the hardware shop was owned by Mr Adams, Martin's father. She loved going shopping there, as there was such a huge range of things, from nails and screws to gardening tools, pet food and kitchen equipment.

Mr Adams was standing behind the counter, sorting out boxes of nails as they entered. "Afternoon, Mrs Hope," he said, looking up as the doorbell rang. "What can I get you today?"

Mrs Hope explained what she needed and Mr Adams went off to fetch it.

"Here's the birdseed," James said to Mandy. They went over to the stand, chose a large packet and took it to the counter, where Mrs Hope was looking at a tray of metal washers.

"How's Emma?" she was saying to Mr Adams. "Settling into her new flat?"

Mr Adams nodded. "It's a bit quiet without her at home. But, seeing as she's only in Walton, she comes back and visits regularly."

"Does she still keep rats?" Mrs Hope asked, picking out a washer.

"Rats?" Mandy said, suddenly interested.

Mrs Hope nodded. "Emma, Mr Adams's

daughter, breeds pet rats," she explained.

"She's got nine adults at the moment," said Mr Adams. "And a litter of six babies. She's giving Martin two of them for his birthday."

Mandy and James exchanged astonished glances. Martin Adams was getting two pet rats!

"Has he got them yet?" Mandy asked, wondering why Martin hadn't mentioned them when Mrs Garvie asked him in assembly that day.

"Emma's bringing them over this evening," Mr Adams told her. He smiled. "He's in the back now, collecting some bits and pieces for them." He turned and called over his shoulder. "Martin! There's a couple of your friends from school here!"

A few seconds later, the curtains leading to the back of the shop parted and Martin edged out. "Hi," he said shyly to Mandy and James.

"I've just been telling Mandy and James

here about your rats," said Mr Adams.

"What are they like?" Mandy was fascinated.

Martin went red. "They're dark grey and white," he mumbled.

"And how old are they?" James asked.

"Are they boys or girls?" Mandy said.

"Six weeks old. And they're both boys." Martin looked cautiously at them from under his long fringe. "Do you like rats, then?"

"We like *all* animals," said Mandy with

a smile. "Don't we, James?"

James nodded.

Martin bit his lip. "Most people like all animals *apart* from rats. They usually think you're weird if you like rats."

"I don't!" said Mandy. "I'd love to have a rat as a pet. I'm not allowed any pets, though, because Mum and Dad are too busy with all the animals that come into Animal Ark." She looked at his worried face. "Is that why you didn't tell Mrs Garvie about getting them as a birthday present in assembly? Did you think people would tease you?"

Martin nodded.

"But that's silly," James burst out. "Everyone at school likes animals."

"Not rats," Martin said. He shuffled his feet. "When I was in Class Two some people in Class Five found out Emma kept rats and they thought it was really odd. They said that rats were dirty and smelly." He pushed back his hair angrily. "But they're not; they're very clean."

"I don't think rats are dirty and smelly," said Mandy, her blue eyes shining. "I think you're really lucky."

"Me too," agreed James.

Martin looked at them, and for the first time his smile seemed really friendly. "Would you like to come and see them?" he asked.

"Yes!" Mandy said eagerly. "When?"

"You could come tonight," said Martin. "Emma's dropping them off at about half past six."

Mandy turned quickly to her mum to ask her if they could go round later. Mrs Hope had caught the end of the conversation. "Yes, of course you can," she said, smiling. "If it's all right with Mr Adams," she added.

"It's fine by me," said Mr Adams cheerfully.

They arranged to meet Martin just before half past six. As they were leaving, Mandy turned back. "Have you thought of names for them yet?" she asked.

Martin grinned. "Cheddar and Pickle," he answered.

2

Cheddar and Pickle

The Adamses' house was at the opposite end of the village to Animal Ark. Before Mandy and James had even got out of the car, Martin was opening the front door. "Come and see Cheddar and Pickle's cage," he said eagerly. "It's all ready for them in my bedroom."

They followed him inside. Mrs Adams was in the kitchen. "Hello," she said, smiling at them. "It's Mandy and James, isn't it?" They nodded. "It's so nice to meet some of Martin's friends," she continued.

Blushing, Martin headed for the door. "We're going to my bedroom, Mum."

They were halfway up the stairs when Mrs Adams suddenly called out, "Martin! Emma's here. She's arrived early."

They all raced back down the stairs. Emma, a tall, slim, nineteen-year-old, was coming up the drive. She was carrying a travelling box with a big blue bow attached to the top. "Happy birthday!" she said, smiling and handing the box to Martin as she reached the door. "Sorry I'm early, but I'm in a bit of a rush."

Martin grinned with delight. "That's all right." He lifted the lid of the box and peered inside. "Oh, wow!" he said softly. Mandy peered over his shoulder and gasped with delight. There, snuggled into a nest of torn-up tissue paper, were two baby rats, each about ten centimetres long. They looked identical. Each had charcoal-grey fur on its head and shoulders, and a white chest and tummy. A mixture of dark-grey and white speckles covered the rest of their bodies. Their noses were pink and they both had little white patches on their foreheads.

"They're gorgeous!" Mandy exclaimed.

"I like their speckles," said James.

"They're called variegated rats," Emma told them. "That means they're a mixture of colours."

Martin beamed at everyone. "This is the best birthday present ever!"

"Shall we take them upstairs and put them in their new cage?" Emma suggested.

They all went up to Martin's bedroom. Against one wall was a large glass tank, just like a big fish tank. Inside, there was a thick covering of shavings on the floor, a nesting-box, a water bottle, and a heavy ceramic dish filled with food. A sturdy ladder leaned against one side of the tank, for the rats to climb up. Martin had also put in two toys – a ball and a wooden block with holes in.

"It's brilliant!" said James, impressed.

"Let's see if *they* like it," said Emma.

Martin very carefully took the lid off the travelling box. He scooped out one of the rats. Looking at it in Martin's cupped hands, Mandy thought it looked just like a very large, very pretty mouse.

"This can be Cheddar," Martin decided.

He was about to put Cheddar into the tank when Emma stopped him. "I've got some shaving from their old cage," she said. "Let me put them in first. That will help them feel at home." She took a plastic bag out of her pocket and scattered the shavings from it into the new cage. "Now put him in," she told Martin.

Martin carefully lowered Cheddar into the tank. The little rat looked around, his whiskers twitching. Then Martin took the other rat out of the travelling box. "This one's Pickle," he said, cradling the rat in his arms. He examined him closely. "Look,

he's got a dark smudge on his nose, so I can tell them apart." He put Pickle into the cage with Cheddar. The brothers sniffed noses and started to explore their new home.

James studied them. "I think Pickle is a little bit smaller, too."

They all looked. 'Yes, I think you're right," said Emma.

"You could bring them into Animal Ark," Mandy suggested to Martin. "Dad often checks out new pets for people."

Emma smiled. "I don't think they really need checking over. They're both very healthy." She glanced down at her watch. "I'm going to have to dash off. I'm meeting some friends in Walton." She picked up a rectangular piece of mesh that was lying on the floor and handed it to Martin. "Remember to keep the cage cover on. You don't want them getting out." She gave him a quick hug. "Happy birthday again. Enjoy them!"

"I will!" said Martin, his eyes shining. "Thanks."

Emma and Mrs Adams went downstairs, leaving Mandy, Martin and James kneeling by the tank. Cheddar went over to investigate the food bowl. Pickle darted round, exploring everywhere, climbing up the ladder and then turning and scampering back down.

"Tomorrow I have to start getting them used to being handled," Martin said. "Do you want to come and help me?"

"Of course!" James said.

"We'd love to," said Mandy with a grin. She watched as Pickle poked his nose inside the wooden block. She thought the two baby rats were wonderful." You should ask if you can bring them into school one day," she said. "I'm sure everyone would love to see them."

Martin looked rather uncomfortable. "I don't want anyone else at school to know about them," he said.

Mandy stared at him. "Why not?"

"They'll think I'm weird," Martin replied.

"They won't. They'll be interested," said James.

Martin shook his head. "No, I'm not telling them!"

Mandy looked at James. She knew that if *she* had two rats she wouldn't be able to *stop* telling people about them. She hoped Martin would change his mind. It would be so much fun if he brought them into school for everyone to see.

Mrs Adams called up the stairs. "Mandy, your mum's here!"

On the way back to Animal Ark, Mrs Hope dropped James off at his house. "See you tomorrow!" he called, wheeling his bike up the drive to his house.

"At eleven o'clock," said Mandy.

When she and her mother got back to Animal Ark, they found Mr Hope filling baked potatoes for supper. He brought them to the table crammed with cheese. Mandy carried through a bowl of salad and sat down. She couldn't stop talking about Cheddar and Pickle.

"I suggested that Martin brought them round to see you," she said to her dad. "But Emma thought he didn't need to."

Mr Hope nodded. "Emma's probably right. Rats are hardy creatures. Did they look happy and lively?"

Mandy nodded. "They've got really shiny coats and bright eyes."

"Then there's no reason for Martin to

bring them in," said Mr Hope. "The important thing for him to remember is that a busy rat is a happy rat."

Mandy frowned. "What do you mean?"

"Well, rats are very intelligent and they need things to keep their minds occupied. They have to have things to do."

"I'd better tell Martin tomorrow," said Mandy. "He did have a ball and a wooden block in their cage, but it might not be enough."

Mrs Hope tucked into her baked potato. "Rats do make very good pets," she said thoughtfully. "They're clean, intelligent and very affectionate. It's shame more people don't keep them."

"Martin says lots of people don't like rats." Mandy sighed. "He doesn't want anyone at school to know about Cheddar and Pickle because he thinks they'll tease him."

Mrs Hope looked concerned. "He's not going to have much fun trying to keep them secret all the time."

"I know," Mandy said. She knew how much her other friends at school loved talking about their pets. It would be a shame for Martin to miss out.

"But you've got friends with hamsters, gerbils and mice as pets, haven't you?" said Mr Hope, helping himself to a huge dollop of butter. Mandy nodded. "And *they* don't get teased," he said. "Rats aren't that different."

"They're more intelligent and more affectionate," said Mrs Hope. "I think you should try to change Martin's mind."

Mandy nodded. "Maybe James and I *will* be able to persuade him," she said thoughtfully.

Mr Hope's eyes twinkled. "If anyone can, you two can!" he said.

Mandy and James met up outside Martin's house the next morning. "I think we should try and get Martin to tell people at school about Cheddar and Pickle," Mandy said.

James nodded. "Definitely. But how?"

"I'm not sure," said Mandy. "We've just got to make him realise he wouldn't be teased."

Martin opened the door. "Hi!" he said. They followed him up to his room. Cheddar and Pickle were awake and exploring their tank. One of them sat up to wash his paws and face, his little hands scrubbing quickly behind his ears.

Mandy checked his nose. No black smudge. "That's Cheddar, isn't it?" she said to Martin.

"So *that* must be Pickle," said James, looking at the other little rat, who was gnawing a piece of wood.

"Rats need to chew on things to keep their teeth short," Martin told them. "You can give them lots of different things – wood, nutshells, dog chews."

"Dog chews?" said James.

Martin grinned. "Yes. Rats love chews." He took off the cage's cover and reached in for Cheddar. "I've been getting them used to being held. They really seem to like it." The little rat sat in his cupped hands. Martin gently stroked behind his ears and Cheddar started to lick his fingers. "They like the taste of salt on our skin," Martin explained.

"Do rats ever bite?" asked Mandy.

"Hardly ever," said Martin. "Not as often as other pet rodents like hamsters and gerbils. Here, do you want to hold him?" he offered.

Mandy reached out and carefully took Cheddar. The little rat's fur was soft and sleek. The tiny claws on his feet dug into the palms of her hand, and he looked round with his intelligent, bright eyes. "People at school with gerbils, mice and hamsters don't get teased," she said to Martin. "You should tell people. I bet they'd be really interested."

James nodded. "Think how much everyone likes Harvey and Terry and Jerry," he said. These were Class Four and Five's classroom gerbils.

"And everyone helped with the harvest-mouse count when we did that at school," added Mandy. She was thinking about the time the school had kept count of the number of harvest mice living near the riverbank.

There was a pause. Martin sighed. "Rats are different," he said.

"They're not really!" Mandy insisted. "And just think how much fun it would be talking about them to people."

Martin looked at her. His eyes were undecided and for one moment Mandy thought he was going to give in, but then he shook his head. "No, I don't want people to know," he said. He picked up a plastic container from beside the tank, unscrewed the lid and took out a raisin. "Let's start teaching them their names."

"But, Martin—" Mandy began.

"All Emma's rats come when they're called," Martin said, interrupting her. Mandy sighed and gave in. He was obviously determined to change the subject. Persuading him to tell people would just have to wait until another time.

"You teach them by using a titbit," Martin explained. "Can I have Cheddar?" He put Cheddar down on the floor and held out the raisin. "Here, Cheddar! Cheddar, come here!"

The rat looked over, saw the raisin and scampered over to Martin, who praised and stroked him. "If you do that often enough they soon learn to come when they hear their names," he told Mandy and James.

"It's just like training a dog to come," said James.

Mandy grinned. "Let's hope they learn quicker than Blackie, then!" Blackie was James's Labrador puppy. Mandy and James had been trying to train him since he was very little. He wasn't very obedient, but he was still adorable.

"What sort of treats do rats like?" James asked.

"Raisins, peanuts, bits of cereal, dog-biscuits, yoghurt and chocolate drops," Martin replied.

Both rats were soon scampering quite happily up to him whenever he called them and held out a titbit. After a while, Martin picked them up and put them back in their cage. "It's really important not to do the same thing for too long," he explained. "Otherwise they get bored. They are very intelligent animals."

"Dad said that rats need to be kept busy," Mandy said, remembering the conversation from the night before. "You'll have to think of lots of things to keep them amused."

Martin grinned. "That's not going to be a problem. Come and see Emma's old bedroom." He put on the cage cover so Cheddar and Pickle couldn't escape, then went out of the door.

Mandy and James followed him curiously. He stopped outside a room further down the landing. "Look at this!" he said, pushing open the door.

Mandy and James stared. There, taking up the whole of one bedroom wall, was an enormous arrangement of plastic pipes and wooden platforms.

"What is it?" gasped James.

Martin turned and grinned. "This," he said, pushing back his fair hair, "is the Incredible Rat Run!"

3

The Incredible Rat Run

Mandy and James investigated the "Incredible Rat Run". Martin pointed out a wooden platform at one end. "You put the rat here," he said. "Then he goes into this pipe, runs down it, and goes up and along this pipe here." With his finger he traced the rat's long, twisty route through the maze of pipes. "Finally he comes out here and crosses the finishing line," he said, showing them a wooden platform at the far end that had a little flag with "Finish" written across it.

"It's amazing!" said James. "Who made it?"

"My dad and Emma. Emma designed it and Dad got the pipes from his shop. It was much smaller to start with, but they gradually made it bigger."

"What are these for?" Mandy asked. She was pointing at several places in the pipes where a round porthole had been cut, just large enough for a rat to get through. Outside each porthole was a small wooden platform.

"They're for putting treats on when you're training the rats to run through it," Martin explained. "You start by putting a titbit on the first platform. The rat runs along the pipes, gets to the porthole and eats the titbit. Then, when he's done the first bit OK, you put the titbit on the second platform so he has to run a bit further."

"When are you going to try Cheddar and Pickle in it?" Mandy asked.

"Emma said to wait for them to settle in first," Martin replied. "But then I'll use it all the time. I'm going to time them with a stopwatch and let them have races."

"Rat races!" said James, grinning.

Martin nodded. "But first they have to

get more used to being handled. Let's go and get them out again."

Mandy and James spent the whole morning playing with Cheddar and Pickle. As they headed back to Animal Ark for lunch, Mandy suddenly had an idea. "We could get Cheddar and Pickle a present. Mrs McFarlane sells dog chews. Why don't we stop off and buy one?" Mrs McFarlane ran the village post office. It sold almost everything.

"Good idea!" said James. "I've got my pocket money with me."

They stopped outside and leaned their bikes against the wall. Mandy often thought the post office was like an Aladdin's cave, the shelves were crammed with so many different things. Whatever anyone wanted, Mrs McFarlane always seemed to have.

James had his hand on the door handle when he suddenly turned to Mandy. "Oh no," he whispered. "Look who's inside!"

Mandy peeped through the glass of the door. A large lady wearing a flowery pink dress was standing by the counter. She held a Pekinese dog under one arm. On her head was a hat, quivering under the weight of the plastic fruit perched round its brim.

"Mrs Ponsonby!" said Mandy. For a moment she wondered if they should give up the idea of getting a dog chew. Mrs Ponsonby was one of the bossiest people in Welford and loved telling everyone what to do.

James was obviously thinking the same thing. "We could come back later," he suggested, but just then Mrs Ponsonby turned and saw them. It was too late. There was no escape.

"Good morning, James. Good morning, Mandy," she said, opening the door.

"Hello, Mrs Ponsonby," said Mandy. She smiled at the fluffy Pekinese. "How's Pandora?"

"Very well, thank you. Aren't you,

sweetheart?" Mrs Ponsonby said to the little dog. Pandora snuffled in reply. She looked rather hot, clutched in Mrs Ponsonby's arms.

"And what have you come in to buy?" Mrs Ponsonby asked, fixing them with a look over the spectacles perched on the end of her nose. "Something educational, I hope."

"Well, actually we came in to buy a dog chew," said Mandy, looking at Mrs McFarlane.

"A rawhide one?" Mrs McFarlane asked. Mandy and James nodded and Mrs McFarlane took down a box of dog chews. They chose one. "How is Blackie?" Mrs McFarlane asked James.

"Oh, it's not for Blackie," he replied, taking out his money. "It's for our friend's two rats."

There was a shriek from behind them. They swung round. "Rats!" screeched Mrs Ponsonby, a hand fluttering to her chest. "Did you say *rats*?"

Mandy nodded. "We've got a friend who has a couple as pets," she said.

Mrs Ponsonby clutched Pandora even tighter. "Pet rats! How awful." She shuddered in horror. "Dirty, revolting creatures!"

"They're not!" Mandy exclaimed.

The fruit on Mrs Ponsonby's hat wobbled as she glared at Mandy through her glasses. "They most certainly *are*!" She put her nose in the air. "Why, if I ever saw a rat at Bleakfell Hall I'd call the rat–catcher the very same day!"

Mandy's blue eyes flashed angrily. James hastily shoved the money on to the counter and, grabbing Mandy's arm, dragged her out of the shop.

Mandy was still angry as she got on to her bike. "How could Mrs Ponsonby say such awful things?" she exclaimed hotly.

James shrugged. "You know what she's like," he said. "It's no use arguing with her." He set off down the road towards Animal Ark. "Let's just hope she never sees Cheddar and Pickle," he called over his shoulder.

Mandy glared once more in the direction of the post office and then cycled after him. Horrid Mrs Ponsonby!

Mrs Adams seemed very pleased to see them when they arrived at Martin's house the next day. "Back again?" she said with a smile. "It is nice to see Martin having friends round for a change. You know, I wanted to organise a birthday party for him, but he insisted he didn't want one." She called into the lounge. "Martin! Mandy and James are here!"

Martin came running through. "Hi!" he said.

"We've brought Cheddar and Pickle a present," said Mandy, giving Martin the dog chew.

Martin grinned. "Thanks!" They followed him upstairs. As they went into his bedroom, the two rats came over to the side of their tank to say hello. They stood up on their back legs and sniffed inquisitively.

"What are we going to do with them today?" Mandy asked.

"I want to let them explore my bedroom," Martin replied. "They need to get used to feeling safe out of their cage. That way they'll be confident enough to explore the rat run when we put them in it." He removed the cage cover, took Cheddar out and put him down on the floor. Cheddar stayed still, his whiskers twitching. "Go on," said Martin, giving him a little push. "Have a good nose around."

Cheddar bounced forward, looked round and dashed back to Martin. He peered round cautiously and then scampered out again. He got a little bit further, then raced back to the safety of Martin's knee.

"He doesn't seem to want to explore," James said.

"He will," Martin replied. "He just needs time to get used to being out of his cage." Sure enough, as the minutes passed, Cheddar began to get bolder. He explored the outskirts of the room, but never stayed away too long before returning to Martin for a cuddle.

When they tried Pickle, he was much more adventurous. As soon as Martin put him down he ran to the middle of the room, stood up on his hindlegs to look round and then scampered over to the bookcase. After a bit, he came running back to Martin, but he didn't stay close for long. Soon he was off exploring again. He climbed up on to Martin's bed, ran along the duvet cover and came down again. He stopped to investigate the electric cable attached to Martin's bedside light.

"No!" exclaimed Martin, clapping his hands.

Pickle jumped and ran back. "He's got to learn not to chew things like that," Martin explained. He looked down at Pickle in concern. "I hope I haven't frightened him, though."

"I think it would take more than that to frighten Pickle," chuckled Mandy, as the adventurous rat jumped down from Martin's knee and set off to explore underneath the desk. He sniffed around some pencils and pieces of paper Martin had left on the floor, and then scuttled up the chair leg and sat on the chair.

After a short time, Martin took a peanut

out of the treat jar. "Pickle, come here!"
The little rat bounced over and took the
peanut in his front paws. Sitting on his back
legs, he looked at them over the top of the
nut, his eyes bright and intelligent as he
nibbled.

"He's going to love the Incredible Rat
Run," said James.

"They're both going to love it," Martin
said. "Rats like challenges." He took
Cheddar out of the tank and put him up

on his left shoulder. "And, as well as teaching them the rat run, I'm going to teach them to ride on my shoulder," he said. "Then they can come everywhere with me." Cheddar snuggled in next to Martin's cheek. "See, he likes it."

Mandy looked at Pickle, who was now darting round the bedroom again. "I can't imagine Pickle staying up there for long," she laughed.

"I think Cheddar and Pickle are going to be good at different things," Martin agreed.

Cheddar licked Martin's ear and looked at Mandy. *I like it up here*, he seemed to say.

"Rats are very interesting," James said to Mandy, as they cycled home. "I wish we could do a project about them at school." He grinned. "Then Martin would *have* to bring them in."

Mandy stared at him. His words had reminded her of her homework project. She'd been so busy thinking about Cheddar and Pickle that she had forgotten all about it. "My maths project!" she said. "What am I going to do it on?"

"When have you got to decide by?" James asked.

"I need to have started doing my recording by Saturday," Mandy replied.

"That's six days away," James said. "You'll easily think of something good by then."

But by Friday Mandy still hadn't thought of an idea that she really liked. At break-time, she started to think about the different things James had suggested. She knew she was running out of time and was going to have to make a decision soon.

"Mandy!" It was Martin. He came running up. "I'm going to try Pickle and Cheddar in the rat run tonight," he told her, his eyes shining. "I rang Emma last night and she said it would be fine."

Mandy immediately forgot about her maths project. "Can James and I come round?" she asked.

Martin nodded. "Come at about half past four." He saw a group of Mandy's friends approaching, and hurried off. Mandy wondered what Cheddar and Pickle would think about the rat run. She could hardly wait until half past four to find out!

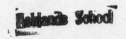

4

Rat race

Martin carried Cheddar and Pickle's cage very carefully through to Emma's bedroom. "They need to learn the run section by section," he explained. "First of all we just want them to get to the first porthole and platform."

"Should I put a treat there?" Mandy

asked eagerly. Martin nodded. Mandy unscrewed the treat jar and placed a peanut on the first platform. The first section of tubing was see-through so they could see the rats running along it.

Martin looked into the tank. "Who should we try first?"

"Pickle," James said. "He's the most adventurous."

Martin put Pickle on the starting platform. As soon as he let go, Pickle scampered forward into the tunnel opening. He hesitated, then his nose twitched as he caught the scent of the peanut waiting on the first platform. He sniffed eagerly, hurrying forward. In a few seconds he had reached the porthole. Jumping on to the platform he ate the peanut.

Martin picked him up. "Let's try that again," he said, "and see if he's any faster."

Pickle was much quicker the second time round. He sniffed the air, then raced through the tubes to the porthole to get his treat. After one more go, Mandy moved the titbit along to the second wooden platform.

When Pickle reached the first platform he stopped, looking confused, but then he caught the scent of the treat waiting a bit further on. Putting his head down, he scampered through the tube and made it to the second platform.

"Clever boy!" said Mandy, who was waiting there for him.

"We should give him a rest now so he doesn't get bored," said Martin, once Pickle had eaten his treat. They swapped the two rats over. Then, after Cheddar had learned to run along the first two sections, they swapped back to Pickle again. Pickle seemed to be much quicker at learning it than Cheddar. But by the end of the training session both of them could make their way from one end of the run to the other.

Martin opened the drawer of the desk and started to rummage around.

"What are you looking for?" James asked.

"This!" said Martin, pulling out a stopwatch. "Emma said she had left it here. We can use it to time Cheddar and Pickle as they go through the run. We'll start with Pickle."

They put Pickle on the starting platform and placed a yoghurt drop on the finishing platform. "Right," said Martin, holding the stopwatch. "Let see how long he takes."

Pickle got from one end to the other in eighteen seconds. They swapped the two rats over. Cheddar was slower; he stopped and started more and took twenty-three seconds.

"Do you think Cheddar will catch up with Pickle?" James asked Martin.

Martin nodded. "Yes. They should both get much faster. Emma had a rat once who could do it in nine seconds. That's the rat-run record."

"We can write their times down," said Mandy, "and see how much faster they get each day."

James stared at her. "That's it!" he exclaimed. "Mandy! That's what you can do!"

Mandy was confused. "What do you mean?"

"For your maths project! Why don't you record Cheddar and Pickle's times over the next fourteen days? You can see how much quicker they get each day."

Mandy's eyes widened. It was a brilliant idea. "Oh, yes!" she gasped.

Martin frowned. "What are you talking about?"

Mandy quickly explained about her maths homework project. "I've been trying to think of something to do for it. Recording Cheddar and Pickle would be wonderful." She noticed Martin's panicky face. "What's the matter?"

"You'd have to tell everyone at school about them," Martin said.

Mandy stared at him pleadingly. "But, Martin, they'll want to hear about them. They'll be interested, *really* they will." Now

James had given her the idea of recording Cheddar and Pickle, she desperately wanted to do it.

Martin looked torn.

"Go on, Martin," urged James. "Let Mandy do it."

Martin gave in. "OK," he said reluctantly. "But if I get teased . . ."

"You won't! Oh, thank you!" cried Mandy, her eyes shining with delight. "It'll be brilliant, Martin. You'll see!"

On Monday morning, Mrs Todd went round the class asking everyone about their maths projects.

"I'm counting how many cars come past my house between half four past and quarter to five each day," Richard Tanner told the class.

"I'm recording the temperature at four o'clock each day," said Andrew Pearson.

Mandy waited impatiently. No one else's ideas seemed to be as interesting as hers.

She couldn't wait to see what everyone would say.

"And Mandy?" said Mrs Todd, reaching her at last. "What about you?"

"I'm recording how long it takes two rats to run through a rat run each day," Mandy said. As she had expected, everyone in the class looked immediately interested.

"Two rats!"

"Who do they belong to?"

"What sort of rat run?"

Mrs Todd smiled at Mandy. "I think you'd better tell us about your project."

So Mandy told everyone about Cheddar and Pickle and the Incredible Rat Run. "I'm going to see how fast they can go," she explained. "Pickle is always faster at the moment, but we hope that Cheddar will catch up."

People called out questions. Mrs Todd clapped her hands. "If you want to find out more you'll have to ask Mandy at break. It sounds very interesting. Well done for coming up with such an unusual idea,

Mandy. I look forward to seeing the results."

Mandy smiled happily and sat down. As soon as she went outside at break-time, she was surrounded by a group of people asking questions. Tina Cunningham, Paul Stevens and Amy Fenton from Class Four joined the group to see what was going on.

Mandy spotted Martin coming out of his classroom with James.

"There's Martin," she said, and waved at him to come over. "They're his rats. He can tell you more."

Martin came over looking nervously at the group of people.

"Mandy says you've got pet rats!" Tina exclaimed. Martin nodded.

"Wow!" said Amy, who had a white mouse called Minnie. "What are they called?"

"Cheddar and Pickle," he told her, almost whispering the names. Mandy noticed a blush creeping over his face.

"Rats are really smelly and dirty," Tina said, wrinkling her nose and looking round for support.

"They're not," Mandy said quickly.

"And they bite," added Tina.

Martin frowned. "No they don't!" He glared at Tina. "Rats hardly ever bite. And they're very clean – they groom themselves several times a day. They're friendly and intelligent and make really good pets."

Tina looked a bit uncomfortable.

"What colour are they?" Amy asked him.

"Grey and white," said Martin. "They're variegated rats."

The questions flowed thick and fast. How old were the rats? What did variegated mean? What did they eat? Where did Martin keep them? As Martin answered the questions, he began to lose his shyness.

"Rats sound like brilliant pets!" said Andrew Pearson, as Martin told everyone how Pickle and Cheddar would come when they were called, and how they liked sitting on his shoulder as he walked round.

Mandy looked at James with relief. It didn't look as though Martin was going to regret telling people at school about his rats after all!

From then on, Martin was stopped every day in the playground by people wanting to know how Cheddar and Pickle were getting on. There was always good news to tell as both rats were getting faster at going through the run all the time. On Thursday, Pickle got from one end of the run to the other in just nine seconds.

"He's equalled the rat-run record!" said James.

"And if he's faster again tomorrow, he'll beat it," said Martin, picking Pickle up. "You're very clever," he told the little rat. Pickle's bright eyes sparkled. *I know*, he seemed to say.

The next day, feeling very excited, they got the rats out. Martin put Pickle on the starting platform. "Eight seconds," he whispered to the little rat. "You can do it!" Pickle looked eagerly into the tunnel.

"On your mark," said James, who was holding the stopwatch. "Get set. *Go!*"

Martin let Pickle go and the little rat streaked off down the pipes. "Here he comes!" said Mandy, a few seconds later. "Stop!" she called to James as Pickle dashed past the flag. James clicked the button on the stopwatch.

"Well?" asked Martin eagerly.

James looked at the stopwatch and looked up, disappointed. "Nine seconds," he said. "The same as yesterday."

They tried twice more, but each time Pickle took nine seconds.

"Maybe he just can't go any faster," James said.

Martin frowned. "I bet he can. We'll try again tomorrow."

Although it was Saturday, Mandy didn't go round to Martin's until the afternoon of the next day. She was busy helping out in the waiting-room with the animals who had come in for morning surgery. Mandy wasn't allowed to help in the actual treatment rooms until she was twelve, but Mandy was allowed to talk to and comfort all the patients that came in. She tried to keep them and their owners as calm and happy as possible.

Richard Tanner from her class had brought in his Persian cat, Duchess, for her vaccinations. Mandy tickled Duchess through the wire front of the pet carrier. The Persian cat stared back snootily.

"How are Pickle and Cheddar?" Richard asked.

"We're going to see if Pickle can break the rat-run record today!" Mandy told him.

"Good luck!" Richard said. "Tell me on Monday how it went."

After surgery was over, Mandy helped to mop up and tidy the waiting-room. Then, getting on her bike, she cycled over to Martin's house. He came to the door to let her in.

Mrs Adams stopped them as they were running up the stairs. "Can you try and keep the house tidy today, please?" she asked. "I've got Mrs Ponsonby coming round later on. I'm trying to persuade her to let the Welford Musical Society use her house, Bleakfell Hall, for a concert, so please don't make too much noise while she's here."

"We won't," said Martin, setting off up the stairs.

"And Martin," Mrs Adams said. Martin looked round again. "Maybe it would be a good idea not to say anything about the rats to her. I'm not quite sure how she would react."

Martin nodded. "OK."

Mrs Adams smiled. "Thanks, love. I really do want her to let us use the hall."

"Mrs Ponsonby doesn't like rats *at all*," Mandy told Martin, as they ran up the stairs. She quickly told him about the time she and James had met Mrs Ponsonby in the post office.

Martin looked alarmed. "We'd better keep them well out of her way, then."

They had just finished setting up the run when James arrived.

"Fingers crossed for the record!" he said.

But, when they tried Pickle through the run, the little rat took nine seconds again. Feeling rather disappointed they put Pickle back in his tank and took out Cheddar.

"Let's see how he does today," said Martin.

Mandy opened the treat jar. It was almost

empty. "I think we need some more treats," she said, putting Cheddar back into the tank, they all went down to the kitchen.

"Mmm," said James, sniffing the air.

Mrs Adams was by the sink. She smiled. "Help yourself," she said, pointing to a wire rack where a batch of freshly baked scones was cooling. "But then make yourselves scarce, Mrs Ponsonby will be here any minute."

Martin quickly collected an assortment of treats from the cupboard while Mandy found three plates and put a scone on each one.

The doorbell rang. "Mrs Ponsonby!" Martin exclaimed, grabbing a plate. "Quick. Let's escape!"

As they reached the top of the staircase they heard Mrs Adams open the door. "Mrs Ponsonby," she said. "*Do* come in."

"Phew!" said James, "Just in time."

They hurried along the landing and into Emma's old bedroom, where they had

left the rats. Mandy was just ahead of the others. Suddenly she stopped dead. "Look!" she gasped. There, sitting in the middle of the floor, was Cheddar!

"The cage cover!" Martin exclaimed, looking at the empty cage in horror. "We forgot to put it on!"

5

Escape!

James quickly scooped Cheddar off the floor, put him back in his cage and positioned the cover firmly in place. Mandy and Martin looked round.

"Where's Pickle?" Mandy asked in alarm.

They started to hunt round the room. James looked under the bed, Mandy checked behind the wardrobe and the chest of drawers, and Martin crawled round on his hands and knees – but there was no sign of Pickle.

"He's not here!" Martin said at last.

James looked out along the landing. "And all the other bedroom doors are shut," he said.

"So where is he?" said Martin.

Mandy heard the clink of china downstairs as Mrs Adams carried a tea tray through to the sitting-room. A horrible thought crossed her mind. Pickle was very greedy and could smell a treat a mile off. She turned to the others. "You don't think Pickle has gone downstairs, do you? He could have smelled the scones."

James and Martin stared at her in horror. "Downstairs?" said Martin.

James gulped. "With Mrs Ponsonby!"

They looked at one another. "Quick!" they all gasped, then raced down the stairs. "Let's look in the kitchen first!" said

Mandy, her heart thudding. "That's where the scones are."

They looked round the kitchen. There was no sign of Pickle. "Ah, good," Mrs Adams said, coming into the kitchen and picking up a plate of scones. "While you're here, you can help me carry some stuff through to the sitting-room. Martin, will you bring the plates; Mandy, the butter and jam; and James, the knives and napkins." She looked sternly at Martin. "And be polite to Mrs Ponsonby!"

"But, Mumm—" began Martin.

Mrs Adams stopped and frowned. "Yes?"

"Nothing," Martin said helplessly.

"You don't have to stay," said Mrs Adams. She obviously thought Martin was unwilling in case he had to talk to Mrs Ponsonby. "Just come and say hello. Then you can escape." She smiled. "I promise."

Shooting worried looks at each other, they followed Mrs Adams into the sitting-room. Mrs Ponsonby was sitting on the sofa wearing a powder-blue dress with large red flowers printed all over. She wore a matching blue hat with a bright-red feather. Sitting on her lap was Pandora.

"Good afternoon, children," she said graciously.

"Hello, Mrs Ponsonby," they said.

"Give Mrs Ponsonby a plate, Martin," said Mrs Adams, but Martin wasn't listening. He was looking round frantically for Pickle. James nudged him and he jumped. "What?" he said, confused.

"I said, give Mrs Ponsonby a plate," repeated Mrs Adams, frowning at him. She turned and smiled at Mrs Ponsonby. "I do hope you like scones, Mrs Ponsonby."

"Yes, I do," said Mrs Ponsonby. She smiled fondly down at the Pekinese on her knee. "And so does my darling Pandora." The dog snuffled happily as she caught a whiff of the delicious scones.

Martin put the plate down on the table in front of Mrs Ponsonby and tried to peer round the corner of the sofa. Mrs Ponsonby stared at him. "What *are* you doing?"

"Martin!" hissed Mrs Adams.

Martin jumped back. "Umm, sorry."

Mrs Adams quickly offered Mrs Ponsonby the scones. "Thank you," said Mrs Ponsonby, taking one for Pandora and one for herself. She daintily cut open the scones and turned to the little dog on her knee. "Now, who's been a good little dog and deserves some delicious scone?" she cooed.

Mandy's eyes suddenly widened. There,

running round the back of the armchair, was Pickle! She gasped. Mrs Adams and Mrs Ponsonby looked at her.

"Mandy?" said Mrs Adams, looking at her in concern. "Are you all right?"

Mandy managed to pull herself together. "Fine," she gulped. She glanced at James and Martin, then stared meaningfully at the armchair. "I think I'll just sit down over there." She edged towards the chair.

"Me too!" said James.

"And me!" added Martin, realising what Mandy had seen.

"What, *all* of you?" said Mrs Ponsonby. "On *one* chair?"

"Martin!" said Mrs Adams. "What *is* going—"

"Grrrrrr," Pandora suddenly growled.

Mrs Ponsonby almost dropped her knife. "Pandora, darling!" she exclaimed in alarm. "What is it?" She looked round frantically.

"Grrrrrr," Pandora growled again, staring at the armchair. Mrs Ponsonby followed her gaze. Mandy, Martin and James hastily tried to block her view.

"Mrs Adams!" Mrs Ponsonby declared, trying to peer round them. "Pandora has seen something by your armchair! Please investigate immediately."

"It's probably just a spider or something," said Martin.

"A spider!" exclaimed Mrs Ponsonby, the feather on her hat quivering.

"Yes, I'm sure I saw one earlier," stammered James. "A really big one."

Mrs Adams looked at them all standing in front of the armchair. "Something's going on," she said sharply. "What are you hiding?" Marching over, she took hold of the chair.

"No, Mum!" gasped Martin.

But Mrs Adams took no notice. She pulled the chair back. Mandy shut her eyes and waited for Mrs Ponsonby's screams.

There was silence.

"There's nothing there," she heard Mrs Adams say in surprise. Mandy opened her eyes. Mrs Adams was right. There was nothing behind the armchair. Pickle had disappeared.

"Oh, Pandora," cooed Mrs Ponsonby. "Have you been teasing Mummy? What a naughty little dog you are."

Mandy's sharp eyes suddenly caught sight of a grey and white shape running along beside the sofa. She grabbed James and Martin and they watched in horror as Pickle scampered up the back of the sofa and started running along the top. He stopped by Mrs Ponsonby's hat. For one awful moment Mandy thought he was about to jump on to the brim. "No!" she cried, leaping forward and grabbing the hat from Mrs Ponsonby's head.

Mrs Ponsonby shrieked loudly. Pandora started to yap. Alarmed at all the noise, Pickle leaped off the back off the sofa and fled for safety, along the floor and through the door. James and Martin raced after him.

"Amanda Hope!" screeched Mrs Ponsonby. "*Whatever* do you think you are doing?"

Mandy stood helplessly, the huge hat in her hands. "I'm sorry," she stammered. "I . . . I . . . I thought I saw a spider fall on your hat!"

"A spider! Well, where is it then?" demanded Mrs Ponsonby, peering through her spectacles.

Mandy looked down at the hat. "I . . . um . . . I must have imagined it."

For once, Mrs Ponsonby was almost speechless. "You . . . you *imagined* it! Mrs Adams, I have never known such behaviour in all my life!"

Mrs Adams took the hat from Mandy. "I think you'd better go and join the others, Mandy," she said firmly.

Mandy fled, thankfully.

"I'm terribly sorry," she heard Mrs Adams saying to Mrs Ponsonby. "I really don't know what has got into the children today. I can assure you they don't normally behave in such a manner. Please, do sit back down and have another scone."

Pickle had run all the way back upstairs

and into Martin's room. "Thank goodness!" said Mandy, when she saw him in Martin's hands.

"How was Mrs Ponsonby?" asked James.

"Dreadful," said Mandy.

"Well, at least she hasn't left," said Martin, hearing his mum go through to the kitchen and put the kettle back on. "Though I don't know what Mum is going to say when she's gone."

"It was funny though, wasn't it?" said James, grinning. "Mrs Ponsonby's face when you grabbed her hat!"

Mandy started to giggle. Martin joined in, and soon all three were gasping with laughter.

"I'm glad you three think your behaviour is so funny," said Mrs Adams, coming up to find them after Mrs Ponsonby had gone. They were still grinning every time they thought of it.

"I'm sorry, Mum," said Martin, looking worried. "Isn't Mrs Ponsonby going to let you use Bleakfell Hall?"

"It's all right." Mrs Adams smiled. "Luckily for you, despite everything, she said yes. Now, would someone like to tell me exactly what was going on down there."

Martin told his mum the whole story and even Mrs Adams saw the funny side of it. "Oh dear," she said, laughing. "Poor Mrs Ponsonby. If only she knew!"

6

A good idea

Over the next few days, neither Cheddar nor Pickle got any quicker at going through the rat run. Mandy recorded their times every day for her graph, but Pickle was stuck on nine seconds and Cheddar was two seconds behind him. Martin puzzled over ways to encourage them. "Maybe we could try having an extra-special treat at the finish," he suggested on Tuesday, when James and Mandy met at his house after school. "Something really sweet. Rats love sweet things."

They went down to the kitchen. It smelled of warm honey and oats. On the table were two wire racks laden with golden squares of freshly baked flapjack. "Perfect!" Martin exclaimed, looking at Mandy and James. "It's sweet, and it's got nuts and oats and raisins. All Cheddar and Pickle's favourite things!"

Mrs Adams came in. "Help yourselves," she said, seeing them looking at the flapjack. "But it's still quite hot, so be careful." They took a piece each and hurried up the stairs. "If this doesn't make Pickle run fast, nothing will!" Martin grinned.

As soon as they took Pickle out of the cage, he sniffed the air eagerly. Mandy put him on the starting platform and Martin placed a tiny piece of warm flapjack just over the finishing line. Pickle could smell it and was so keen to run that Mandy had a struggle to hold him back.

"Here goes," she said to Martin and James.

James set the stopwatch. "On your mark, get set, go!" he called. Mandy let go of Pickle. The little rat flew through the tunnel, and as he crossed the finishing line James pressed the stopwatch button. He looked at the time and frowned. "Ten seconds," he said.

"But that's a second slower!" Martin exclaimed.

They were very puzzled. Pickle seemed to love the flapjack, eating up every last scrap and cleaning his paws afterwards. They tried him again, but he was no faster.

"That's strange," said Mandy. "He's never got *slower* before."

"Maybe he's just having an off day," James suggested.

Martin nodded, relieved. "He'll probably be faster again tomorrow."

But the next day, Pickle took eleven seconds. "I don't understand it," said Martin, taking him down from the finishing platform.

Mandy was concerned. "Do you think he's OK?" she asked. She looked closely at the little rat, but his coat seemed as shiny as always and his eyes were just as bright. "Is he eating properly?" she asked Martin.

"He's eating lots," Martin replied. "he never seems to stop."

Mandy ran her hand over Pickle's sides. His ribs were well-covered. "He *is* a bit plump," she said. "Maybe he needs to go on a diet."

Martin shook his head. "Emma said that rats should never be put on a diet while they're growing. But we could cut his treats down a bit."

"We could break them up into smaller pieces," James suggested.

Mandy nodded, and looked at Pickle again. Maybe he was running slower because he'd put on a bit of weight. She tickled his ears. Hopefully that was all it was and he would soon be running at top speed again.

But cutting down his treats didn't seem to work. In fact, Pickle got even slower. By Thursday Mandy was really getting worried. "There must be something wrong with him," she said to Martin as they took the little rat down from the finishing platform. "Perhaps you should bring him into Animal Ark and let Dad have a look at him."

"But he doesn't seem ill," said Martin. "Surely if he was ill he would be quiet and off his food."

"Martin's right, Mandy," said James. "Pickle looks healthier than ever!"

Mandy looked at Pickle's shining coat and bright eyes. She had to admit that James and Martin were right. She frowned. So why was he going so slowly?

"Have you brought in your graph?" Sarah Drummond asked Mandy the next morning.

Mandy nodded. Mrs Todd had asked them all to bring in their graphs so she could have a look over them. When she saw Mandy's, she was very interested to see that Pickle had slowed down although Cheddar's times had stayed the same. She held the graph up so everyone in the class could see. "Look at how the line on the graph goes down as Pickle gets slower," she told them.

"Why is he getting slower?" Jill Redfern asked.

"I don't know," Mandy admitted.

"Perhaps Pickle doesn't like going in the run," said Sarah.

Mandy shook her head. "He gets really excited when it's his turn to have a go. We have to hold him back to stop him running before the stopwatch is ready."

"Maybe he's not well," suggested Richard Tanner.

"He doesn't look ill," said Mandy. "And he's eating lots." She glanced round to see if anyone else had any suggestions, but they looked as puzzled as she felt.

Mrs Todd smiled at her. "Well, it looks like you've got a mystery on your hands, Mandy. It'll be interesting to see if you can solve it."

"It's a rat riddle!" said Sarah.

Mandy sat back down. Sarah was right, it certainly was a riddle. There had to be some reason why Pickle was getting slower.

She frowned. If only she could work out what it was.

Mrs Todd clapped her hands, interrupting Mandy's thoughts. "Your finished graphs are due in on Monday, together with a written description of what you have found." She turned and smiled at Mandy. "Maybe you'll have solved your mystery by then, Mandy."

Mandy nodded. She hoped so.

"You're very quiet tonight," Mr Hope said to Mandy as she helped him set the table for supper. "Is there something on your mind?"

Mandy sighed. "It's Pickle," she said, putting down the knife and fork she was holding. It had taken Pickle fourteen seconds to get through the run that evening.

"Anything I can help you with?" asked Mr Hope.

Mandy explained about Pickle getting slower and slower. "He used to be so fast," she said. "But now he's even slower than Cheddar."

Mr Hope frowned. "How does he seem in himself? Is he lively and eating well?"

Mandy nodded. "He looks healthier than ever. His coat's really shiny at the moment and he's really greedy."

Her father scratched his beard. "It doesn't sound like he's ill, then." He looked suddenly thoughtful. "You say Pickle always used to be the fastest through the run?"

Mandy nodded.

"And did he learn how to complete the run quite quickly?" Mr Hope asked.

"He learns everything really quickly," Mandy replied. "Much quicker than Cheddar." She felt suddenly hopeful. "Do you think you know why he's getting slower, Dad?"

"I do have an idea," Mr Hope replied. He smiled. "Pickle sounds like a very intelligent rat to me. I suspect he's just bored with the run."

"Bored!" Mandy echoed.

Mr Hope nodded. "The more intelligent a rat is, the more it needs new challenges and situations," he explained, going to the cupboard to fetch some plates. "Maybe you should try and change the run. You could make it longer. Or, even better, set up two possible routes and choose a different one for him to do each day."

Mandy threw her arms round him. "Oh, Dad, that's a brilliant idea!" Her eyes shone. She had never thought there would be such

a simple solution "Can I ring Martin?"

Mr Hope nodded, his eyes twinkling. "Go on, but be quick. Mum will be home soon and she'll want her supper."

Mandy ran to the phone. Martin thought that extending the run was a brilliant idea. "I'll talk to Dad," he promised, "and see if he can bring some more pipes home from the shop. We can put in more bends and turns and maybe even some obstacles!"

"We can plan it out tomorrow," said Mandy. The next day was Saturday and they would have lots of free time. "I'll ring James and tell him to think up some good ideas."

She made another phone call to James. When she came back through to the kitchen, her eyes were shining. Mr Hope was stirring a pan of pasta. "You look a bit happier," he said, smiling.

Mandy grinned. "Pickle isn't going to be bored any more. We're going to make him the most exciting rat run that's ever been seen!"

7

Stuck!

When Mandy and James arrived at Martin's house the next day, they found Martin almost bursting with news. "Dad says he's got a whole load of pipes at the shop we can have! He's going to bring them home tonight and help us rebuild the run tomorrow!"

"We should make some plans," said James. "Draw out exactly what it should look like."

Martin found a large piece of paper and spread it on the desk in his bedroom.

"We could make it so there are two different routes the rats could take," Mandy suggested.

"And I think there should be some extra things," Martin said. "What about making some ladders? Rats can be trained quite easily to run up ladders for food."

"And what about putting in a few little doors?" James said. "Like cat-flaps that the rats can push open."

"Good idea," said Martin. He picked up a pen. "Let's draw it."

Soon the piece of paper was filled with their drawing of the extended rat run. There were tunnels and doors and ladders.

"It looks brilliant," said Mandy, sitting back to admire it.

"I'll go and ring Dad," said Martin. "I'll tell him what we need."

While he was gone, Mandy and James took Cheddar and Pickle out of their tank. "I'm so glad there isn't anything wrong with Pickle," said Mandy, cradling him in her arms.

"Two healthy rats," said James, passing Cheddar from one hand to the other. He looked critically at Pickle. "Although Pickle is still looking rather fat."

"He is, isn't he?" Mandy agreed. "Still, once we have the run sorted out, he'll soon lose weight with all the exercise."

James grinned. "There's going to be loads to make. I think tomorrow's going to be rather busy!"

"But fun!" added Mandy with a grin.

The next morning, Mr Adams set about organising them to help him with the task of rebuilding the run. He was wearing old, dusty clothes and had a pencil stuck behind his ear. "Now, Martin, you make the cat-flaps," he said.

"Or, rather, rat-flaps," Martin said to Mandy and James.

Mr Adams handed James a bag full of long, thin pieces of wood, together with a ruler, glue and a small saw. "These are for the ladders," he said. "They need to be twelve centimetres long and three centimetres wide. Have you used a saw like this before?"

James nodded. Mandy's grandad had showed him how to use carpentry tools when they had built a go-kart together.

"We need six ladders," said Mr Adams.

"Measure out the wood first, James, then cut it up using the saw. When everything is cut, I'll help you stick the rungs on the ladders using a hot glue gun."

"What can I do?" Mandy asked eagerly.

"Can you help me with the pipes, Mandy?" said Mr Adams. "We need to unscrew some of the pipes that are already in place, attach new ones and work out where we need new portholes."

They all set about their tasks. "These are different pipes from last time," said Mandy, picking out a white plastic pipe from the pile on the floor. It was about forty centimetres long.

Mr Adams nodded. "They're a little bit narrower and longer, but they were the only ones I had spare. They'll be fine." He examined the run. "Right, let's start by unscrewing this section here."

At lunch-time, Mrs Adams came up with a tray of sandwiches and hot tomato soup in mugs. They put down their tools.

"This is delicious," said James, taking a

huge bite of a ham sandwich. "Thanks, Mrs Adams."

"What do you think, Mum?" asked Martin. The pipes had now been changed and extended. The ladders and doors were in the middle of being fixed into place.

"Very impressive," said Mrs Adams. "When do you think it will be ready to try out?"

"Another couple of hours, I reckon," replied Mr Adams.

Mandy grinned excitedly at Martin and James. She couldn't wait to see what Cheddar and Pickle thought of their new run.

It was four o'clock before the run was finally ready. It now filled at least half of the bedroom. Mr Adams stood back, shaking his head as he looked at the maze of pipes, ladders and doors. "That is certainly some rat run," he said.

"It's the Ultra-Incredible Rat Run now," said James, laughing.

Mr Adams smiled, and took his toolbox

downstairs. Martin carried Cheddar and Pickle's cage through and put it down on the floor. "We'll have to teach them the way through it first," he said.

"Let's start with Pickle!" said Mandy in excitement.

Martin carefully took Pickle out of the cage and put him on to the starting platform. There were now two tunnels the rats could go down, but for now one of them was blocked off. Pickle sniffed the new white pipe, looking rather surprised.

"We'll just get him through to the first ladder," said Martin.

James opened the jar of treats and put a piece of biscuit on the platform by the first ladder.

"Just a small piece," Mandy reminded him. Judging from Pickle's round tummy, she could tell that two days with no exercise had done him no good at all.

"Here goes," said Martin, letting Pickle go. Pickle set off down the tunnel. Mandy and James waited eagerly at the first platform, but the rat didn't appear.

They waited a bit longer. "Where is he?" asked James, puzzled.

"Pickle!" Mandy called.

But still there was no sign of the little rat.

"Can you see him, Martin?" she asked. But Martin, who was still at the starting platform, couldn't see Pickle.

"Do you think he's just stopped?" asked James.

Mandy's eyes widened. "What if he's got stuck?" she said, in alarm.

They looked at one another in horror.

"I'll get Dad!" said Martin.

Martin raced downstairs and returned with Mr Adams. "Now, what's all this?" Mr Adams said. They quickly explained.

"Pickle *has* been getting fatter," said Mandy. "And the pipes are narrower than before."

Mr Adams frowned and started to unscrew the sections of pipe. "I'll go slowly," he said. He unscrewed one, then another, and then . . .

"There's Pickle!" cried Mandy.

She could just see the little rat's nose. His whiskers were twitching frantically. His ears were pressed to the side of his head.

"He's stuck!" Mandy gasped.

Mr Adams, Martin and James all clustered around the pipe. Martin held out a biscuit. But Mandy was right – Pickle was stuck fast!

Mr Adams scratched his head. "If we unscrew more of the pipe, maybe we'll be able to tip him out."

"Be careful with him, Dad," said Martin anxiously as Mr Adams twisted the tube round.

"Poor Pickle!" said Mandy. The little rat looked terrified. His eyes were wide with fear.

Mr Adams carried the tube over to the desk. It was about forty centimetres long. Near one end they could just see Pickle's nose. Mr Adams gently tipped the tube up and patted the end, but Pickle's fat, round body was holding him fast.

"What are we going to do?" Martin cried.

Mr Adams looked worried. "I don't know. Maybe we should ring Emma to see if she has any ideas." He hurried off.

Mandy crouched down and looked into the tube. "It's all right, Pickle," she soothed. "We'll get you out."

Martin was almost in tears. "What if we can't?"

"We will," said Mandy. "Emma will know what to do." But inside she wasn't

quite so sure. She waited anxiously. When Mr Adams came back, she saw immediately that he wasn't looking any happier.

"Well?" Martin demanded. "What did Emma say?"

Mr Adams shook his head. "She didn't know what to do. She's never had a rat stuck in a tube before. She said we'd better take him to the vet's. She's going to meet us there."

"Should I ring Dad?" Mandy asked. "To let him know that we're coming in?"

"If you would, Mandy," said Mr Adams, running a hand worriedly through his hair. "The phone's in the hall."

Mandy ran down the stairs. Mr Adams, Martin and James followed more slowly with Pickle.

Mandy dialled the Animal Ark number. After a few rings, her dad answered. "Hello, Animal Ark. Adam Hope speaking."

"Dad, it's me." Mandy quickly explained about poor Pickle.

"Now, don't worry," said Mr Hope, his

voice calm and reassuring. "I have to say it's unusual for a rat to get stuck, but bring him in and we'll work out a way to free him. Try to keep him as calm as you can, Mandy."

Mandy ran to the car. "Dad's waiting," she told them.

"Hop in, then," said Mr Adams, who had the engine running already. "Let's not waste any time."

Mandy got into the back of the car beside James. Martin was cradling the tube in his arms in the front seat. "It's all right, Pickle," he said. "We'll get you out of there."

Mandy's heart thudded in her chest as she looked at the frightened rat shivering in the pipe. Poor Pickle. How exactly *were* they going to get him out?

8

The riddle solved

Mr Hope was waiting for them as they hurried into Animal Ark. He took the tube from Martin. "Right, let's see what we have here." He looked in both ends of the tube. "You are in a bit of a state, young fellow, aren't you?" he murmured. "I think we'd better get you out of there as soon as possible."

He carried the tube through to one of the treatment rooms, studied it for a moment, then turned to Mandy. "Mandy, could you get me the rolling-pin from the kitchen, please."

"The rolling-pin?" asked Mandy, in astonishment.

Mr Hope nodded. "The thin wooden one, without handles."

Mandy ran off to the house. When she returned with the rolling-pin, she saw that her dad had put out a large piece of foam and some parcel tape. James, Martin and Mr Adams were all looking mystified. Mr Hope quickly wrapped the foam round one end of the rolling-pin and secured it with tape. "Now, I just need a saw," he said.

"A saw!" Martin gulped.

"Back in a minute," said Mr Hope, as he left the room. He returned a few minutes later carrying a small handsaw.

"It's all right," Mandy said, seeing

Martin's face. She thought she knew what her dad was going to do. "He's going to cut the tube to make it easier to get Pickle out. Aren't you, Dad?"

Mr Hope nodded. "I'm going to cut it off here," he said, pointing to a place a few centimetres in front of Pickle's nose. "Then I'm going to try and push him out using this." He held up the rolling-pin, its end now covered with soft foam padding. "Mandy, if you could hold the tube for me please."

Mandy held the tube firmly on the table as her dad quickly and carefully sawed off the end. The end of the tube dropped off and they could see Pickle's nose and whiskers almost poking out. Mr Hope put on a pair of heavy leather gloves and took the tube from Mandy.

"Now, be careful," he warned. "When Pickle does come out, he might be scared and may bite."

"Pickle wouldn't bite!" said Martin.

"Not in normal circumstances,"

explained Mr Hope, "but when an animal is frightened it tends to react without thinking. It's far better to be safe than sorry." With one hand half-covering the front end of the tube, he carefully put in the rolling-pin and started to push very gently.

At first, nothing happened. Then Pickle's whiskers started to appear at the end of the tube. "He's coming out!" Martin exclaimed.

Pickle's nose emerged, and then his head

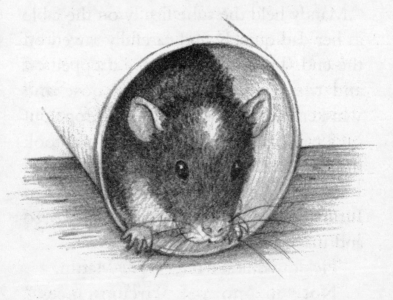

and shoulders. "Here he comes!" said Mr Hope. He pushed a bit harder and the little rat popped out.

"He's free!" cried Martin, as Mr Hope caught him in his glove.

Scared stiff, Pickle scrabbled and panicked and tried to escape, but Mr Hope held on. "There, there, little fellow," he soothed, cupping him in the leather gloves. The little rat gradually calmed down. He poked his nose out of the gloves and looked at everyone.

"Oh, Pickle!" said Martin, overjoyed.

"Is he all right?" Mandy asked anxiously.

Mr Hope removed one of the gloves and began to examine Pickle. He ran his hands down his legs and felt him all over. Suddenly he frowned.

"What is it, Dad?" Mandy asked, her heart leaping into her mouth. Mr Hope turned Pickle upside down and examined him underneath.

"He *is* OK, isn't he?" Martin said.

"Pickle is fine," said Mr Hope, turning

Pickle the right way up again. His eyes twinkled suddenly and a smile caught at the corners of his mouth. "There's only one problem. Pickle isn't a he. He's a she, and . . ." he handed the little rat back to Martin, "she's pregnant."

"Pregnant!" gasped Mandy.

"Pregnant!" exclaimed Martin.

Mr Hope nodded. "How old is Pickle now, Martin?"

"He's . . . I mean, *she*'s nine weeks old," said Martin.

"Surely that's too young to be pregnant?" frowned Mr Adams.

Mr Hope shook his head. "I'm afraid not. Rats can get pregnant from about seven weeks old, and it looks as if that's exactly what Pickle has done. I would say the babies are due in about five days."

"Oh, wow!" said Martin, looking down at Pickle in delight. "I'm going to have baby rats." He shook his head in disbelief. "Amazing!"

Just then, there was a knock at the door. Emma poked her head round. "I got here as fast as I could," she said anxiously. "How is he? Is he all right?"

Everyone looked at each other. "I think you'd better come in," said Mr Hope.

When Emma heard that Pickle was pregnant, she gasped. Her hand flew to her mouth. "I was in a bit of a hurry that night," she admitted. "I must have picked out the wrong rat. Oh, goodness! I'm really sorry, Martin."

"*I* don't mind." Martin grinned. "I think it's brilliant!"

Mr Hope smiled. "I think Cheddar and Pickle are going to have to live separately from now on," he said. "Rats can get pregnant again immediately after giving birth."

"I'll get you a new cage," Emma promised Martin.

"Will the babies be all right?" Mandy asked worriedly.

Mr Hope nodded. "They should

be fine," he said. He turned to Martin. "Just give Pickle as much food as she wants to eat, and keep her quiet from now on."

"No wonder Pickle has been getting slower going through the rat run," said James. "We thought she was just eating too much!"

"Or that she was bored," added Martin.

Mandy grinned. She'd never imagined that this would be the solution to the rat riddle. "Just wait till I tell Mrs Todd!" she said.

Mandy and James cycled to school on Monday morning talking constantly about Pickle. Mandy's completed maths project was in her schoolbag.

"Look, there's Martin!" said James, seeing him walking up to the school gates with his mum.

They cycled over. "How's Pickle?" Mandy asked, getting off her bike to wheel it up the path.

Martin grinned. "She's fine. I can't wait till she has the babies."

Mrs Adams shook her head. "I couldn't believe it when Martin told me Pickle was pregnant."

Amy Fenton was walking past with Paul Stevens. They stopped. "Pickle's pregnant?" said Amy, looking surprised. "But I thought he was a boy!"

"So did we all," said Martin with a grin. "There was a bit of a mix-up."

"When is she having them?" asked Paul.

"What? Is Pickle having babies?" said Richard Tanner, walking up with Andrew Pearson.

Soon there was a crowd of people gathered around Martin. He told them the whole story about Pickle getting stuck in the tube. Mandy looked at him standing in the middle of the crowd, his eyes shining as he talked. To think that at the beginning he hadn't wanted anyone at school to know about Cheddar and Pickle . . .

"I never knew Martin had so many

friends," Mrs Adams said in a surprised voice to Mandy and James.

"He didn't really, until he told everyone about his pet rats," James said.

Mrs Adams looked puzzled, so Mandy explained.

"So *that*'s why Martin didn't want a party on his birthday," Mrs Adams said. She looked thoughtfully at Mandy and James. "Do you think he'd like a surprise party now? I always thought it was a shame he didn't have one on his birthday."

"I think he'd love it!" said James.

"If it was after the babies are born it could be a birthday party for them as well," added Mandy.

"I'd need some help organising it, if it's to be a surprise," said Mrs Adams.

James turned to Mandy. "We'll help, won't we, Mandy?"

Mandy nodded. "Of course!"

Two and a half weeks later, on a Friday evening after school, Mrs Adams dropped

Martin off at Mr Adams's shop in Walton. Mandy and James had given party invitations to lots of people in Class Four and Class Five, and at five o'clock, thirty people arrived at Martin's house. They helped put up balloons, set out the tea table and made a pile of presents. Mrs Adams had invited Mr and Mrs Hope. Mr Hope couldn't be there because one of them had to stay at Animal Ark, but Mrs Hope had come to help.

"He should be back any minute!" said Mrs Adams, carrying a beautifully iced birthday cake in to the sitting-room. It was shaped like a giant grey and white rat.

"Quick, hide!" said Mandy, seeing Mr Adams's car draw up outside.

Everyone ran and hid. Mandy and James crouched behind the door in the kitchen. They could hear a few giggles. "Shh!" said Mandy, but that made people want to giggle even more. Paul Stevens snorted as he tried to swallow a laugh.

They heard the front door open.

"Mum," called Martin. "We're back."

"*Surprise!*" shouted everyone, jumping out and throwing streamers.

Mandy burst out laughing at Martin's astonished face. "It's a late, late birthday party!" she said.

Mrs Adams came hurrying through. "Happy birthday, love," she said, giving him a hug.

Martin looked round at all his friends and the balloons. "Wow!" he said in disbelief. "*Wow!*"

"Come on, have a look at your presents!" said Tina Cunningham, and she and Paul dragged him through to the sitting-room. Mandy grinned at James. It looked like Martin's party was going to be a great success.

It was. And the highlight of the whole party came after they had all eaten. "Can we see the babies?" asked Amy Fenton, as Mrs Adams handed out slices of birthday cake.

Martin ran upstairs and came back down

carrying a large, new cage. Everyone
cleared a space and he put it down on the
floor.

"Oh, look!" gasped Tina. "Aren't they
sweet?"

There were six babies in the tank. They
looked just like Cheddar and Pickle, each
one having a dark-grey head and a speckled
body. Their eyes had just opened and they
blinked round at everyone. They were tiny,
but perfect in every way.

Martin smiled down at them proudly.

Mandy and James watched everyone cluster round.

"They're gorgeous!"

"Have you got homes for them?"

As Mandy watched Martin showing off his rats to his friends, she felt a hand on her shoulder. She turned to look at her mum. "Happy now?" Mrs Hope asked softly.

Mandy grinned. The riddle was solved and, because of his rats, Martin had made lots of new friends.

"Oh yes!" she said.

LUCY DANIELS
Animal Ark Pets

0 340 67283 8	Puppy Puzzle	£3.50	☐
0 340 67284 6	Kitten Crowd	£3.50	☐
0 340 67285 4	Rabbit Race	£3.50	☐
0 340 67286 2	Hamster Hotel	£3.50	☐
0 340 68729 0	Mouse Magic	£3.50	☐
0 340 68730 4	Chick Challenge	£3.50	☐
0 340 68731 2	Pony Parade	£3.50	☐
0 340 68732 0	Guinea-pig Gang	£3.50	☐
0 340 71371 2	Gerbil Genius	£3.50	☐
0 340 71372 0	Duckling Diary	£3.50	☐
0 340 71374 7	Doggy Dare	£3.50	☐
0 340 73587 2	Frog Friends	£3.50	☐
0 340 73588 0	Bunny Bonanza	£3.50	☐
0 340 71373 9	Lamb Lessons	£3.50	☐
0 340 73585 6	Donkey Derby	£3.50	☐
0 340 73586 4	Hedgehog Home	£3.50	☐

All Hodder Children's books are available at your local bookshop, or can be ordered direct from the publisher. Just tick the titles you would like and complete the details below. Prices and availability are subject to change without prior notice.

Please enclose a cheque or postal order made payable to *Bookpoint Ltd*, and send to: Hodder Children's Books, 39 Milton Park, Abingdon, OXON OX14 4TD, UK. Email Address: orders@bookpoint.co.uk

If you would prefer to pay by credit card, our call centre team would be delighted to take your order by telephone. Our direct line *01235 400414* (lines open 9.00 am–6.00 pm Monday to Saturday, 24 hour message answering service). Alternatively you can send a fax on *01235 400454*.

TITLE		FIRST NAME		SURNAME	

ADDRESS	
DAYTIME TEL:	POST CODE

If you would prefer to pay by credit card, please complete:
Please debit my Visa/Access/Diner's Card/American Express (delete as applicable) card no:

Signature .... Expiry Date: ....

If you would NOT like to receive further information on our products please tick the box.   ☐